PECOS BILL PRESENTS PECULIAR PANHANDLES

Maryland Tales

Clinton Lloyd Oberbeck

Clover Fields Press

Copyright © 2025 Clinton Lloyd Oberbeck

All rights reserved.

The characters and events portrayed in this book are fictitious. Any similarity to real persons, living or dead, is coincidental and not intended by the author.

No part of this book may be reproduced, or stored in a retrieval system, or transmitted in any form or by any means, electronic, mechanical, photocopying, recording, or otherwise, without express written permission of the publisher.

Paperback ISBN: 9798306914084

Published by Clover Fields Press, an imprint of OUI, LLC.
CloverFieldsPress.com
Amarillo, Texas

CONTENTS

Title Page
Copyright
Foreword
Chapter 1: The Great Cryptid Contest   1
Chapter 2: The Hagerstown Ghost Light   5
Chapter 3: The Lost Treasure of the Potomac River   10
Chapter 4: The Sideling Hill Phantom   15
Chapter 5: The Mysterious Mount Savage Shadows   20
Chapter 6: The Catoctin Mountains Snallygaster   24
Chapter 7: The Haunting of Antietam Battlefield   28
Chapter 8: The Wills Creek Trickster   32
Chapter 9: The Veiled Lady of Williamsport   36
Chapter 10: The Phantom Train of Western Maryland   40
Chapter 11: The Sometub Voyage on the C&O Canal   44
Chapter 12: The Savage River Reservoir Monster   48
Chapter 13: The Dogmen of the Allegany Mine   53
Chapter 14: The Appalachian Wendigo   57
Chapter 15: The Disappearing Gandy Dancer   61
Chapter 16: The Maryland Heights Ghost   66
Chapter 17: The Cacapon River Serpent   70
Chapter 18: The Banshee of Washington County   74

Chapter 19: The Legend of the Dewayo	78
Chapter 20: Reflectin' on the Maryland Panhandle	82
Sneak Peak	85
About The Publisher	87
About The Author	89

FOREWORD

I reckon I've seen my fair share of wild and wondrous things, from the backwoods of Kentucky to the deep rivers of the Ohio Valley. But when I heard about Pecos Bill—heck, I couldn't pass up the chance to tell y'all a little about what it means to be a river man, a legend, and someone who's got a real kinship with the wild side of life.

Now, you might think Pecos Bill is just another tall tale—another cowboy spinning stories in the wind—but let me tell you, I've met a lot of folks like him. He's got that same spark that comes from having wrestled with the river, faced down the wild, and laughed in the face of danger. Just like me, he knows that the world's full of creatures and things that can't be explained, but that's part of the fun, isn't it? It's all about looking the unknown square in the eye and saying, "You may be bigger than me, but I ain't afraid of you."

What Pecos Bill does in these stories is just that—he faces the odd, the mysterious, and the downright strange head-on. From the ghostly trains running on tracks long abandoned to creatures that walk the night like they own it, Pecos rides into each tale with his boots on the ground and a grin on his face. But that's the way it is when you're a true legend—when you're made of stories that get bigger and wilder with every telling.

I may not be the one ridin' through the Maryland Panhandle, but I sure can appreciate a good adventure. And if you're lookin' for one, you're in the right hands with Pecos Bill. So sit back, relax, and hold on tight. You're in for a wild ride filled with ghosts, beasts, and a whole lotta Pecos Bill-style humor. And remember—don't take it too seriously. The best legends, after all, are meant to be enjoyed, not explained.

Now, if you don't mind, I'll be back on the river. But don't go too far—there's plenty more adventure to be had in these stories. Trust me on that.

Yours in Legend,
Mike Fink

CHAPTER 1: THE GREAT CRYPTID CONTEST

It was a dark and misty evening deep in the Appalachian foothills of the Maryland Panhandle. The kind of night where the fog rolls in so thick you can't see your own boots, let alone any cryptids lurking around. But tonight, that's exactly what was going to happen.

You see, in the deepest, foggiest parts of the woods, a peculiar event was about to unfold. The cryptids of Maryland had gathered for the first-ever Great Cryptid Contest of the Maryland Panhandle. From the Snallygaster to the Dewayo, the Wendigo, and even the mysterious Dundee Devil, every strange creature had come out of hiding for one reason—to see who could win the coveted title of Maryland's Most Mysterious Creature. And who better to judge this competition than me—Pecos Bill, a man who's wrangled more legends than most folks would dare to dream about.

I stood there, at the edge of an overgrown clearing, looking at the contestants. It was a full moon night, so you could make out a few glowing eyes in the distance and hear the rustling of claws on the ground. Let me tell you, folks, the cryptids here were a motley crew, each with their own special talents, all eager to win.

"Alright, everyone, gather 'round!" I called out, holding up my hat for emphasis. "It's time to start the contest! First up—we'll have a talent show. Show me what you got, and try not to scare me too much. I'm only human, after all."

The Snallygaster, that terrifying half-bird, half-reptile, with wings that could block out the moon, flapped its wings proudly and strutted forward. It puffed out its chest and screeched so loudly I almost lost my hearing. The audience of cryptids—mostly ghosts, cryptids, and a few odd raccoons—seemed unimpressed. It might have been the wingspan or the fact that Snallygaster sounded like a cat being stepped on.

"Well, that was certainly loud," I said, wincing. "But, uh, maybe tone it down next time? Might scare the other contestants."

Next up was the Dewayo, the wolf-man. The poor creature's fur was looking a little disheveled as it nervously approached the center. It scratched the back of its head with a claw before doing an awkward little dance. I mean, it wasn't exactly Swan Lake, but you had to admire the effort. It wiggled its bushy tail and gave a half-bark, half-woof of encouragement.

"Well, that's what I call a wolf with rhythm," I said with a grin. "But I don't think anyone's gonna be hiring you as a dance instructor."

After the Dewayo came the Wendigo, which decided to

try its luck with a bit of fire-breathing. Now, I had seen a lot in my time, but watching a skeletal creature with glowing eyes attempt to light a match—only to have it fizzle out and set its own fur on fire—was new.

"Now, you've really done it," I said, dodging the flames. "I didn't know fire safety was part of this contest, but maybe we'll consider it next time."

Just as I was about to judge, I saw the Dundee Devil stepping out of the shadows. It was a massive creature, with the body of a wild boar and the head of a goat, horns and all. It gave a gruff snort, then blew out a puff of smoke like it was trying to impress me with some sort of "smoke rings." Instead, it just looked like it had smoked a bit too much chili for lunch.

"Well, if that wasn't the most confusing thing I've seen in the last 24 hours, I don't know what is," I said. "You're an interesting mix of animal, but I think we need to work on that smoke technique."

Finally, it was time for the Glen Burnie Ghost, who floated into the clearing with all the grace of a bedsheet in a windstorm. It glided in a circle and made the most unearthly wailing noise that could've rivaled an owl with a sore throat. But when it tried to lift a pumpkin in the air with its ghostly powers, it dropped it—sending the poor ghost into a fit of wailing and apologizing.

"Well, shoot," I said. "You get points for effort, but let's try something more... controlled, next time."

After all the performances, I stood in the middle of

the clearing, pretending to think it over. I looked at the cryptids, each one holding their breath.

"Well, folks, after careful deliberation..." I began, raising an eyebrow. "I have to say this contest was one for the ages. A lot of talent, a lot of heart, and a lot of fire hazards. But, I reckon there's one winner who really impressed me. The Dewayo with its... unique moves!"

The Dewayo's tail wagged enthusiastically, and the other cryptids groaned in collective dismay. But hey, it was all in good fun.

"And, as for the rest of you," I continued, "you all get honorable mentions for being the most terrifying, confusing, and fire-prone collection of creatures I've ever had the pleasure of judging."

The cryptids scattered off into the night, their growls and howls echoing in the woods, while the Dewayo performed a final celebratory spin.

"Well, partner," I said to the air, "that was one for the books. I'm glad I got to judge that contest—though next time, I'm gonna need a seat further from the fire hazard."

And so ended the Great Cryptid Contest of the Maryland Panhandle, a night where creatures both feared and funny came together under the same foggy sky. As for me, well, I'm off to find the next great adventure—preferably one where fire safety and dance moves aren't involved.

CHAPTER 2: THE HAGERSTOWN GHOST LIGHT

Now let me tell ya somethin'—you won't find many things stranger than the Hagerstown Ghost Light if you're wanderin' around in the Maryland Panhandle. Folks around there like to spin yarns about it, claimin' it's a ghost, a will-o'-the-wisp, or maybe even a cursed lantern lost in time. But if you ask me, it's just another one of those "peculiar" things Pecos Bill can't resist investigatin'. And so, one fine, crisp evening, there I was, ridin' along Route 40, my eyes fixed on the dark, misty hills of the Appalachian Mountains, when I heard the tale of the Hagerstown Ghost Light.

I'd just pulled into town, nothin' but the sound of Widowmaker's hooves clippity-cloppin' on the road, when an old feller with a crooked cane leaned in close. He looked like he might've seen more years than any man should, his voice cracklin' like a dry leaf.

"You goin' to see the light, stranger?" he asked, his eyes narrowin'.

I tipped my hat and gave him a friendly wink. "Might

just. What's the story, old timer?"

He chuckled, spittin' some tobacco on the ground. "The ghost light's been hauntin' these parts for near on a hundred years. Some say it's the spirit of a poor ol' feller who got lost on the railroad tracks. Some folks swear it's a cursed lantern—ain't no one been able to figure it out for sure."

Well, now, that got my curiosity rollin' faster than a tumbleweed in a Texas windstorm. I figured, if it was ghosts and lanterns they were dealin' with, Pecos Bill could sure as shootin' help sort it out.

The moon was just startin' to peek over the hills when I pulled my hat down low and set off in search of the mysterious light. Now, in Hagerstown, people like to tell you it's all spooky, full of fog and shadows, but I've seen my fair share of creepy stuff, and I wasn't about to be spooked by a little mist and a lantern. Heck, I've had cows spookier than that.

I rode Widowmaker through the quiet streets and out past the old railroad tracks where the light was said to show itself. The trees stretched their long arms like they were tryin' to grab at the night, and the only sound was the breeze blowin' through the leaves. But then, out of nowhere, there it was. A faint, flickering light in the distance, bobbin' like a lantern carried by some invisible hand.

Now, I don't scare easy, but even I had to admit—this was a bit odd.

"That's one fancy trick," I muttered, squinting through the fog. I leaned forward in the saddle, curious as a cat in a room full of rocking chairs. I wasn't about to let some ghost or wisp outsmart ol' Pecos Bill.

The light moved closer, and I noticed something strange. It didn't flicker like a lantern—it bobbed up and down like someone was walkin' with it. And that, folks, got my attention more than a rattlesnake in your boot.

"Alright, now," I said to Widowmaker, "let's see what kind of trouble we're walkin' into."

We trotted closer, and I called out, "Hey there! What's goin' on? You lost, or just showin' off your glow-in-the-dark skills?"

The light didn't answer, but it did stop movin' and just hovered there, like it was waitin' for me. I took a deep breath, ready to face whatever this was, and spurred Widowmaker ahead.

As I got closer, I could make out a shape—a tall, shadowy figure, maybe a man, standin' in the glow. The closer I got, the more peculiar it became, like lookin' at a mirage on a hot desert day. I pulled up next to it and shouted, "Alright, mister, this is gettin' mighty weird. What's the deal with the light?"

The figure turned slowly. And I'll be honest, I wasn't quite prepared for what happened next. It wasn't a man at all. No, sir. It was a ghost, alright, but not like any ghost I'd ever seen. This one was flickerin' in and out of existence, all hazy and transparent, with the faint shape of an old railroad conductor's hat perched on its head. The light, it seemed, was comin' from the lantern in his ghostly hands.

"Well, ain't you a sight," I said, grinnin' like I'd just won a poker game. "I reckon you're the one causin' all this ruckus, huh?"

The ghost didn't speak, but it nodded slowly, and the eerie light flickered brighter. Now, I've encountered my fair share of spirits, but this one had the look of someone who didn't quite know he was dead.

"Let me guess," I continued, my voice as smooth as a creek in spring, "you were just tryin' to find your way home and got lost, huh? Too bad you didn't have a map or maybe a good sense of direction."

The ghost sighed, and I could feel the sorrow rollin' off him like a summer thunderstorm. It was clear he was stuck in some kind of loop—walkin' around with that lantern, searchin' for somethin' he couldn't find.

"I reckon I can help," I said, not one to leave a good ghost hangin'. "You need to head toward the light, but not the one you're holdin'. The one that leads you out of here."

I gave him a little wink and nudged Widowmaker forward. The ghost hesitated, but then, like it had finally figured it out, it began to walk away, lantern light fading into the mist.

I tipped my hat and smiled. "Sometimes, all you need is a little help from the right stranger."

With that, the Hagerstown Ghost Light flickered one last time before fading into the distance, leaving me standing in the quiet night, once again ridin' through the peculiar corners of the Maryland Panhandle.

CHAPTER 3: THE LOST TREASURE OF THE POTOMAC RIVER

Well, now, if there's one thing Pecos Bill's good at, it's findin' treasure—or at least findin' the trouble that comes with huntin' it. And when I heard tell of a lost treasure buried somewhere along the Potomac River in the Maryland Panhandle, you better believe I wasn't gonna let it slip by me. I didn't need no fancy map, just a good ol' gut feeling and a horse with the stamina of a thousand jackrabbits.

I'd been spendin' a few days in the area, y'know, tryin' to figure out what made this part of the world so peculiar—'cause, let me tell ya, everything here's a little stranger than a cow in a tuxedo. That's when a feller with a weathered face and a crooked smile told me about the treasure hidden along the banks of the Potomac. Said it was lost after a band of rebels hid it during the Civil War. The feller didn't say much about the treasure's specifics, but he swore it was still out there, waitin' to be found.

"You think it's still there, old timer?" I asked him, takin' a sip of my drink and watchin' his eyes twinkle like he was tryin' to hold back a big ol' secret.

"Oh, I know it is," he replied, nodding slowly. "But you ain't gonna find it without help. The river's got a way of keepin' things hidden, like it's protectin' 'em. You find the treasure, and the river'll take somethin' back."

Well, that sounded just ominous enough for me to take interest, so I packed up my gear and headed for the Potomac River's edge. Now, the river's a mighty thing—big and wide, flowing with a kind of quiet strength that makes you think it's seen more history than any ol' book could ever hold. The further I went, the more the trees seemed to lean over the water, casting long shadows that stretched across the land like they were tryin' to hide the past.

I tied Widowmaker up at the riverbank, the water lappin' against the shore, and set off into the woods. As I walked through the thick underbrush, I kept thinkin' about what the old man had said. The river had a way of hidin' things, huh? Well, that just sounded like a challenge to me.

It wasn't long before I found somethin' strange—a big rock, worn smooth by the water, with a strange symbol carved into its surface. It wasn't no typical settler's mark; it looked older, like it had been there long before anyone started talkin' about treasure.

"Well now," I said to myself, "ain't this peculiar?"

I reached down and ran my fingers over the carving. It was faint, but there was something about it that gave me a shiver up my spine. It was as if the rock was tryin' to tell me somethin', like it was a clue to somethin' bigger.

Just as I was about to investigate further, a voice broke through the silence, echoing from behind me. "You won't find it."

I spun around, hand on my lasso, but I didn't see a soul. The air grew thick, like the river itself was holdin' its breath.

"Who's there?" I called, my voice steady.

From the shadows, a figure stepped forward—a man, his face gaunt and pale, his clothes ragged, like he'd been wanderin' through the wilderness for too long. His eyes were wild, and his voice sounded like it had come from the deepest parts of the earth.

"The treasure's cursed," he said, his words slow and deliberate. "No one who's tried has ever made it out alive."

"Now, I reckon that's a mighty bold claim," I said, narrowing my eyes. "Who are you, and why's this treasure so cursed?"

The man didn't answer at first. He just stared at me, his eyes wild with some kind of fever. Then, finally, he spoke again.

"It was hidden by a band of soldiers during the Civil War," he said. "They buried it here, by the river, and the earth won't let it go. Those who try to take it, the river... it takes them. One by one."

I didn't much care for the sound of that, but Pecos Bill

don't scare easy, so I just shook my head and chuckled.

"Well, I reckon I'm about to make that curse a whole lot less scary," I said, smilin' wide. "You see, if there's treasure to be had, I'm the one to find it."

The man let out a low laugh, like he'd heard this story a hundred times before. "You'll see," he muttered, as if to himself.

I didn't have time to waste on this ol' feller, though. I was there for treasure, not ghost stories. So, I marched right past him, my eyes set on the spot where the symbol was carved.

With a little digging—just the way a man does when he's in a hurry—I found something. A chest, just barely hidden beneath the roots of a massive tree, its iron lock rusted and nearly falling apart.

"Well, I'll be," I said, pulling the chest free. "Looks like ol' Pecos Bill is one step ahead."

But just as I was about to open the chest, a strange chill ran through the air. The river seemed to groan, its waves moving in an odd rhythm, almost like a warning. Still, I wasn't about to back down.

I pried open the chest, and inside—well, it wasn't gold or jewels like I'd expected. Nope. It was a bunch of old maps, dusty and fragile, with more symbols and markings on 'em than I could make sense of.

Just then, the man from before appeared again, his face

twisted with anger.

"You fool!" he shouted. "You've released it! The curse will come for you now!"

I chuckled and waved my hand. "Oh, I think you've been watchin' too many ghost stories. This here's just a map, and I aim to use it to find out what's really goin' on here."

Before he could say another word, I tucked the maps into my coat and headed back to Widowmaker. The river was quiet again, but I couldn't shake the feeling that I'd just set off a chain of events I wasn't quite prepared for.

So, as I rode out of there, with the Potomac flowing peacefully behind me, I couldn't help but think: the treasure wasn't what I'd expected—but it was somethin' just as good. And Pecos Bill wasn't one to turn away from a new mystery.

CHAPTER 4: THE SIDELING HILL PHANTOM

Well, folks, when you're out in the Maryland Panhandle, you're bound to run into some curious things. And that's exactly what I was doin' when I made my way to Sideling Hill. Now, I'd heard tell of a phantom that haunted the slopes of Sideling Hill, a place so remote and rugged it might as well have been the backside of the moon. The locals said it was the ghost of a wagon driver who'd lost his life in a tragic accident many, many years ago. Some folks claim the phantom's a wanderer, lost forever between worlds. Others say he's a protector, keeping anyone from making the same mistake that caused his death.

Me? I wasn't one to put much stock in ghost stories, but I sure as shootin' wasn't about to let a good mystery slip by. So, when the sun started settin' behind the hills, I saddled up Widowmaker, packed a little extra rope, and made my way toward Sideling Hill. I had a feeling that if this phantom wanted to be found, ol' Pecos Bill was the one to do it.

Now, Sideling Hill ain't no easy place to get to. It's steep, rocky, and covered with dense trees that make it look like the land itself is tryin' to hide somethin'. But I wasn't in any hurry to get anywhere else. I've dealt with a few ghosts in my time—some friendly, some not so much—and I wasn't about to let a little spooky mist keep me from uncoverin' what was goin' on.

As I climbed higher into the hills, the air got thicker, the trees grew taller, and the sun's last rays barely touched the ground. A strange quiet settled over the place, like the land was holdin' its breath. That's when I saw it. A shadow, flickerin' in and out of the trees like a wisp of smoke. At first, I thought it was just my eyes playin' tricks, but then, it came closer.

A tall figure appeared before me, walkin' across the rocky path like he didn't even notice me. He was dressed in old-timey clothes, with a long coat and a wide-brimmed hat that shaded his face. He didn't look like he was from around here—more like he belonged to another time, a time when wagons and horses ruled the land.

"Whoa there," I called out, steadyin' Widowmaker with a firm tug on the reins. "You lost, partner?"

The figure stopped in his tracks, slowly turnin' to face me. His face was pale, his features sharp and ghostly, like a man who hadn't seen the light of day in a long time. His eyes, though, were sharp—like he knew somethin' I didn't.

"I'm not lost," the phantom said, his voice cold and distant, like a winter wind. "I'm stuck."

Now that got my attention. I swung down off Widowmaker and took a few steps closer, eyeing the ghost with caution. "Stuck, huh? Well, I reckon I've helped a few folks outta tight spots in my time. You mind tellin' me what's goin' on here?"

The phantom's ghostly figure flickered in the fading light as he looked toward the path ahead. "It was years ago," he said slowly. "A wagon, lost in the hills. I was driving it, headin' to a place I didn't know. The horses spooked, and we went over the edge. The wagon... it was lost, and I... I never made it out."

Now, I'll admit, that sounded like a mighty tragic tale, but I wasn't one to let a ghost wallow in his misfortune. "Well, now, partner," I said, tipping my hat, "sounds like you've been wanderin' these hills a long time. But I reckon there's somethin' I can do about that."

The phantom turned to me, a flicker of something like hope in his eyes. "You'd help me?"

I nodded, my mind already workin'. "I can't promise I'll fix your wagon, but I can certainly help get you back where you belong."

With that, I started lookin' around. Sideling Hill was full of twists and turns, but I figured if this phantom had been wanderin' for years, he might know more about the land than he realized. So, I asked him, "If you could go anywhere, where would you go?"

He didn't answer at first. He just stood there, like he was thinkin' hard. Finally, he said, "To the bottom of the hill. To where it all started."

That was enough for me. I mounted Widowmaker and motioned for the phantom to follow. "Then let's head on down there. Might be we'll find what you've been lookin' for."

As we descended the hill, the land seemed to change. The air lightened, the fog started to lift, and the eerie quiet of the hill began to feel less like a curse and more like a memory. Finally, we came to a small clearing at the foot of Sideling Hill. And there, hidden among the trees, was a wreckage—a broken-down wagon, long forgotten and buried by time.

The phantom stepped forward, his ghostly hand reaching for the remnants of the wagon. As his fingers touched the old wood, he began to glow, his form becoming brighter and more solid. The sadness in his eyes faded, replaced with a look of peace.

"Thank you," he whispered, his voice softer now. "I can rest now."

With that, the phantom's form flickered one last time before disappearing, leaving me alone in the clearing. The night felt different now—lighter, freer, like the hill had let go of its burden.

I tipped my hat and grinned. "Well, now, that's how you solve a ghost problem."

As I made my way back up Sideling Hill, I couldn't help but think that, in this peculiar Panhandle of Maryland, sometimes the biggest mysteries weren't the ones you had to solve—they were the ones that solved themselves.

CHAPTER 5: THE MYSTERIOUS MOUNT SAVAGE SHADOWS

Well, I've seen my share of strange sights, but nothing quite prepared me for the tales that followed me into Mount Savage. Now, you might be thinkin', "Mount Savage? That's gotta be a misnomer," but let me tell ya— when you're in the Maryland Panhandle, even the towns have a way of makin' you question everything you thought you knew.

I'd heard whispers about the shadows of Mount Savage —figures that moved across the mountaintop late at night. Some said they were the spirits of miners, long since gone, still toilin' away in the dark. Others swore up and down that the shadows were somethin' else entirely—demonic shapes that had crawled up from the depths of the earth.

Now, I ain't one to run from a good story, especially when it smells like mystery. So when I rolled into Mount Savage, I wasn't lookin' for peace and quiet. No sir, I was lookin' for those shadows.

I saddled up Widowmaker and made my way to the foot of the mountain, the trees thick around me like they were tryin' to shut me out. The air was colder than a rattlesnake's kiss, and the wind howled like a wolf with a bone to pick. But Pecos Bill don't scare easy. I've ridden through tornadoes, wildfires, and even a stampede of mad bulls, and none of 'em ever got the best of me.

The locals, though, looked mighty nervous when I asked about the shadows. They'd tell ya just enough to make you want to know more, but no one was brave enough to venture up the mountain after dark. I reckon it was too much for even the hardiest folks to stomach.

"Well, if no one else is gonna do it, I reckon I'll give it a shot," I said, makin' my way to the base of the mountain with a grin on my face. Widowmaker snorted, as if to agree, and we started our climb.

As we made our way up the trail, I couldn't help but feel like I was bein' watched. Not by the folks in town, but by somethin' else—somethin' older, darker. The shadows seemed to stretch out longer the higher we went, like they were tryin' to reach for us.

By the time we reached the summit, the sun had dipped low, and the mountain was bathed in the kind of eerie twilight that makes every rock and tree look like a figment of your imagination. That's when I saw it. The shadows, like wraiths, movin' across the ridge. They weren't just the shadows of trees or rocks, though. They were... different. They had form. They had shape.

I pulled my hat lower, squintin' through the gloom. "Alright, I reckon it's time to see just what these shadows are all about."

Widowmaker snorted, his hooves clippity-cloppin' on the rocky ground as I dismounted. I took a few steps forward, careful not to make a sound. The shadows were movin' faster now, almost like they knew I was comin'. I couldn't shake the feeling that they were circlin', waitin' for somethin'.

Then, from behind a large boulder, stepped a figure— tall, thin, and as dark as the night itself. Its eyes glowed faintly, a strange red that seemed to burn through the dark. It wasn't a man. It wasn't a beast. It was something else entirely.

"Well now," I said, tilting my hat back and sizing the creature up. "I reckon you're the one causin' all this fuss?"

The shadow didn't speak, but it did step forward, the ground beneath it cracklin' like it was alive. "You are not welcome here, stranger," it said in a voice that sounded like the wind howlin' through the cracks in the earth.

I grinned. "Well, I didn't come here to be polite, partner. I came to figure out what in tarnation you are."

The shadow flickered, its form wavering like smoke in the wind. "I am the keeper of the mountain. The one who watches over it. You should turn back. The mountain does not want you here."

I chuckled and patted my horse. "Well, I'm here now, and I reckon it's too late to turn back."

With that, I pulled out a coil of rope and started

swingin' it around like I was wranglin' a stubborn steer. The shadow lunged, but I was faster. I cast the rope in one smooth motion, catchin' the creature in midair. It howled as the rope tightened, its form flickerin' and shuddering.

"I don't know what kind of tricks you think you're pullin', but they ain't gonna work on me," I said, yankin' the rope tighter.

The shadow fought, but it wasn't used to bein' tied down. It flickered once more, and then, with a shriek that rattled the trees, it disappeared, leavin' only the eerie quiet of the mountain behind.

I stood there for a moment, catchin' my breath. "Well, that wasn't quite what I expected, but I reckon I got the job done."

The sun had fully set by now, and the shadows of Mount Savage seemed to retreat into the mountain itself. As I mounted Widowmaker and turned toward town, I couldn't help but grin. Another mystery solved, and another strange story to add to the list.

CHAPTER 6: THE CATOCTIN MOUNTAINS SNALLYGASTER

Well, folks, when I heard tell of a creature with the wings of a bird, the body of a lizard, and teeth sharp enough to cut through steel, I figured it was time to saddle up again. They called it the Snallygaster, and the stories from the Catoctin Mountains were enough to make even the toughest folks in the Maryland Panhandle sleep with one eye open.

This here Snallygaster, though, wasn't just some ordinary creature. No, sir. It was said to have the wings of a dragon, sharp claws, and sometimes even tentacles or one big ol' glowing eye. Now, you'd think something that sounded like it came straight outta a fever dream wouldn't bother a man like me, but curiosity got the best of me. Besides, no one had been brave enough to track it down for years, and I wasn't about to let some mystery stay unsolved—especially when it involved a creature that could make a grown man run for the hills faster than a rabbit in a fox den.

So, one evening as the sun began to set behind the trees, I packed up my gear, gave Widowmaker a pat on the neck, and headed toward the Catoctin Mountains. The locals had warned me, said no one had seen the Snallygaster in a long time, but I knew better. If there was a creature in these hills, Pecos Bill was gonna find it.

The further I rode into the mountains, the darker it got. The trees stretched up into the sky like they were tryin' to touch the stars, and the air felt thick, like the whole forest was holdin' its breath. Every now and then, I'd hear a rustle in the trees or a screech in the distance that made the hairs on the back of my neck stand up. But I kept on, determined to find the creature that had haunted these woods for generations.

As the last light of day faded, I heard it—the screech of something big, something that didn't belong. It echoed through the trees, like the call of a bird, but deeper, more guttural. My instincts kicked in, and I followed the sound, pushing through the underbrush.

Then, I saw it. A shadow flitted across the trees, too fast to make out clearly, but there was no mistaking the shape —wings, large and bat-like, flapping through the air like it was as natural as a hawk catching the wind. I crept closer, Widowmaker's hooves silent beneath me, and then I saw it.

The Snallygaster—a creature straight out of nightmare. It was perched on a cliff, its reptilian body glowing faintly in the moonlight. The creature had the head of a bird, with sharp, hooked beak and glowing eyes that seemed to pierce the night. Its wings were folded, but even then, I could see how powerful they were, like they could carry it across the mountains in a heartbeat. And that mouth—well, let's just say you wouldn't want to get too close, 'cause it looked like it could swallow a man whole.

I wasn't sure if I'd been spotted or not, but I wasn't about to stand around and find out. I reached for my lasso, careful not to make a sound. The Snallygaster's head snapped in my direction, its single, glowing eye locking onto me.

"Well now, you sure know how to make an entrance," I muttered, tipping my hat back.

The creature screeched again, this time launching itself into the air with a beat of its mighty wings. It was faster than a hawk on the hunt, but Pecos Bill wasn't about to let it get away. I threw my lasso in a wide arc, and just as the Snallygaster soared past, the rope caught it around the wing.

The creature howled, thrashin' in the air, but I held tight. "You ain't gettin' away that easy!" I yelled, pulling hard on the rope. With one final heave, I yanked the Snallygaster to the ground, sending a cloud of dust and leaves into the air.

It struggled for a moment, but I had it pinned. "Alright, partner," I said, walking slowly toward it, "we're gonna have a little chat about your habits of scaring the good folks around here."

The Snallygaster glared at me with its glowing eye, its claws twitching, ready to strike. But I wasn't about to give up. I tied it down with a few good knots, making sure it *couldn't break free.*

"Now, I don't know what you think you're doin' up here, but I reckon it's time for you to find a new hobby," I said, grinning wide. "Maybe stick to catching small critters instead of makin' people think they've seen the end of the world."

The creature snarled, but the fight seemed to leave it. It was like it knew it was beat. I gave it one last look before untangling the lasso and walking back to Widowmaker.

"Well, that was one for the books," I said to my horse, who just snorted in response.

As I rode out of the Catoctin Mountains, the night was quieter, the trees a little less spooky. And as for the Snallygaster? Well, it wasn't the last I'd seen of it, but for now, it was just another tale for the books—a cryptid captured, a mystery solved, and another day in the peculiar Maryland Panhandle.

CHAPTER 7: THE HAUNTING OF ANTIETAM BATTLEFIELD

Now, folks, if you're talkin' about a place steeped in history, there ain't no place quite like Antietam Battlefield. Situated right in the heart of the Maryland Panhandle, this battlefield's got more history than a Texas cattle ranch, but it's also got somethin' else—a dark, eerie presence that lingers in the air like a storm that never quite passes. When I heard the stories about the battlefield bein' haunted by the spirits of soldiers, I figured it was about time I rode in and took a look for myself.

The day was overcast, like the sky was gettin' ready to break open at any moment, when I rode up to Antietam. You could feel the weight of the land—the history, the lives lost, the battles fought. The place wasn't just a memorial to the past; it felt like the past was still hangin' around, like it hadn't quite let go.

I tied up Widowmaker at the edge of the battlefield and started walkin'. The air was thick, the ground soft and wet from a recent rain, and the silence was the kind that makes you uneasy. I could hear the faint rustling of leaves, but that was about it. The whole place seemed like it was holdin' its breath, waitin' for somethin' to happen.

As I walked further into the field, I noticed a chill in the air, colder than a grizzly's stare. I wasn't the type to be spooked easily, but this place... well, this place had a way of settlin' into your bones. The stories about the ghostly soldiers that roamed the battlefield didn't help either. Some folks claimed to have seen shadows movin' across the field at night, others heard the faint sound of drums and battle cries echoin' on the wind. And then there was the one about the phantom general who appeared at the head of his army, ready to fight a battle that had ended over a hundred years ago.

I was thinkin' about all these stories when I heard it—the sound of footsteps behind me, light but heavy enough to be heard over the wind. I spun around, ready for anything, and that's when I saw him—a figure in a tattered uniform, his face pale and drawn. His eyes were empty, like he was lookin' at somethin' no one else could see.

"Well now," I said, squintin' at the figure, "I reckon you're a bit out of time, partner. This war's been over for a long while."

The ghostly soldier didn't say a word, but his presence felt like a heavy weight in the air. He stood still for a moment, and then, like he'd made a decision, he started walkin' toward me, his boots crunching softly in the wet grass. I didn't back down, though. I stood tall, ready for whatever might come next.

The ghost stopped a few paces away, and for a long

moment, we just stared at each other. Then, he raised his hand, pointing to the ground, where a faint red glow began to pulse beneath the earth. I looked at the glow, confused, and then back at the ghost, who seemed to be waiting for me to understand.

"You're lookin' for somethin', aren't you?" I asked, squinting at the soldier. "Some unfinished business?"

The ghost nodded slowly, and in that moment, I realized what was happenin'. The battlefield wasn't haunted by random spirits—it was haunted by those who still had a score to settle. They were trapped here, stuck between life and death, because their fight had never truly ended.

"Well, partner," I said, adjusting my hat, "I reckon I'm here to help. Tell me what you need, and we'll see if we can't get it sorted."

The soldier lowered his arm and pointed toward the distant woods. Without a word, he turned and began walking, his footsteps barely making a sound. I followed him, my boots crunching on the wet ground as I made my way toward the trees.

As we reached the edge of the woods, I saw it—the remnants of a battlefield that had long been forgotten. It wasn't much, just a few scattered remains, but the air around it felt charged, like the land itself was holdin' its breath. The ghostly soldier stopped and turned to me.

"This is where it happened," he said, his voice barely a whisper. "This is where the battle ended. But not for me."

I nodded, my heart heavy with the weight of the history that had been left behind. "I reckon it's time you got some peace."

I stepped forward and knelt beside the ground, reaching out and touching the soil. The red glow from before pulsed brighter, and I could feel a change in the air—like the land was finally ready to let go.

The soldier gave me one last look, his eyes now clear and full of gratitude. "Thank you," he whispered, before disappearing into the mist.

With that, the battlefield grew quiet again, the air lighter than it had been when I arrived. The spirits of the past had found their rest, and the battlefield, once haunted by the echoes of war, was finally at peace.

I mounted Widowmaker, giving the land one last look as I rode away. The history of Antietam would always remain, but for now, the ghostly soldiers could rest easy.

CHAPTER 8: THE WILLS CREEK TRICKSTER

It was a warm, breezy afternoon when I rode up to Wills Creek, the water flowing clear and swift over the rocks. The fog had cleared up for a change, but something about the land still felt off, like there was a presence watching me from the trees.

Now, I've been through some strange places in my time, and I've met plenty of unusual characters, but when I came across Wills Creek, it was like the land itself was playing a game with me. The trees leaned in close, their branches whispering in the wind like they were gossiping about some old secret. But I wasn't interested in secrets—I was here for adventure, and I wasn't about to let any old trickster spirit get in my way.

That's when I saw him—the man standing at the edge of the creek, with a look on his face like he was trying to hold in a laugh. He had dark, tangled hair and a long, colorful shawl draped over his shoulders, but there was something strange about him—his eyes glimmered, and his smile stretched a bit too wide. He was just standing there, staring at me, grinning like he knew something I didn't.

"Well, partner," I called out, adjusting my hat, "you

gonna stand there all day, or are you gonna tell me who you are?"

The man—if you could call him that—tilted his head and flashed a grin that could've cracked a rock. "I am the Trickster," he said in a voice that echoed in the trees. "I've been waiting for you, Pecos Bill."

I raised an eyebrow. "Now, I don't know what kind of game you're playing, but I reckon I've seen enough mischief in my time. I don't mind a good laugh, but I don't have time to waste."

He laughed then, a sound like leaves rustling in a storm. "Oh, I'm not here to waste your time, Pecos Bill. I'm here to teach you a lesson."

"Teach me a lesson?" I scoffed. "The only lesson I've got time for is how to tame a wild coyote or rope a runaway train."

The Trickster stepped closer, his hands raised in mock innocence. "But Pecos Bill, you don't understand! I've come all this way just to challenge you. You see, I'm the spirit of Wills Creek, and I'll see if I can't teach you a little humility!"

Before I could respond, the ground beneath me shifted. The creek began to ripple, and the wind kicked up as the Trickster spun around, his form blurring in the air like smoke. Suddenly, I found myself standing on the opposite side of the creek, my horse nowhere in sight.

"Well now, I've heard of a good challenge, but this is a

little much," I grumbled, staring at the Trickster, who was now laughing louder than a jackrabbit on fire.

"You'll have to get back across the creek if you want to beat me," the Trickster taunted. "But I've set a little trap. You'll need to be clever!"

I narrowed my eyes. "Clever, huh? Well, I've got plenty of tricks up my sleeve, and if you think you can outwit Pecos Bill, you've got another thing coming."

I took a step toward the creek, but before I could move any further, the water in front of me rose up like a wall, blocking my way. The Trickster was still grinning, his arms crossed over his chest.

"Well, well," I said with a smirk, "I reckon we'll see who's really clever, won't we?"

I grabbed my lasso, aimed it at a tree branch hanging just above the water, and with a flick of my wrist, I swung across the creek, landing lightly on the opposite bank, right in front of the Trickster.

"You didn't expect that, did ya?" I said, tipping my hat. "Now, how about you show me how to play this game for real?"

The Trickster's eyes widened in surprise, then narrowed again with a mischievous glint. "Well, well, you've won this round, Pecos Bill. But this isn't over."

"Not by a long shot," I said, grinning back at him. "But I reckon you've got a lesson to learn, too. Maybe next time, *don't underestimate me."*

With that, the Trickster vanished into the wind, leaving behind a gust of laughter that echoed across the creek. As the wind died down and the creek calmed, I realized that maybe, just maybe, I had learned something myself. The trick wasn't just about outsmarting the spirit—it was about knowing when to stand your ground and when to take a good laugh for what it was.

"Well, partner," I said to the air, "I reckon I'll be back to Wills Creek. But next time, I'll make sure I bring a good sense of humor and a stronger rope."

CHAPTER 9: THE VEILED LADY OF WILLIAMSPORT

It was a cold October night when I found myself riding through the foggy streets of Williamsport, Maryland. I had heard the rumors—the stories of a woman draped in black, a Veiled Lady who wandered the streets after dark. Some said she was a ghost, others said she was a phantom born of the town's dark history, but one thing was certain: she terrified the folks around here, especially when the Halloween season rolled around.

Now, I've dealt with ghosts, cryptids, and all manner of strange things in my time, but this one? This was a new one for me. I'd seen plenty of spooky stuff, but a woman who walked the streets cloaked in black with clawed hands and a chilling wail? Well, partner, I couldn't resist checking it out.

I rode into town as the sun dipped below the horizon, casting the streets into shadows. The buildings here were old, and the cobblestone streets felt like they had a mind of their own, twisting and turning through the fog. I tied up Widowmaker outside a local tavern where a few townsfolk had gathered, nervously glancing at the windows.

"Pecos Bill!" one of 'em called out. "Are you here to find that Veiled Lady?"

I tipped my hat and gave 'em a smile. "That's the plan, partner. A good ghost story's always worth investigating."

"Well, just be careful," said the man, his voice shaky. "She's been causing a stir again. Folks are whispering that she'll be out tonight."

As I walked through the streets, I could feel something in the air—like the whole town was holding its breath. I'd been in plenty of spooky situations, but there was something unsettling about this place. The fog rolled thick around the corners of the buildings, and in the distance, I heard it—a faint, mournful wail, like the wind had turned into a woman's voice.

I turned a corner and nearly bumped into her. There, standing in front of a house, was a tall woman draped in black, her face completely hidden by a veil. Her hands, long and clawed, reached out as though she was beckoning me forward. Her eyes—though I couldn't see them—seemed to burn with an eerie light beneath the veil.

"Well now," I said, tipping my hat, "I reckon you're the Veiled Lady, huh? You've got the look, that's for sure."

The lady didn't say a word—just stood there, the veil swaying with the wind. The wail that had been in the air seemed to come from her very chest, sending a chill through the night.

I took a step forward. "I'm not easily scared, lady. But I'd appreciate it if you gave me a good reason not to laugh at this little act of yours."

The lady reached forward with her clawed hand and grabbed the front of my shirt, pulling me closer. Her eyes —those glowing, fiery eyes—seemed to burn into me, but I didn't flinch.

"Well, that's a little rude," *I said, raising an eyebrow.* "If you're lookin' for a fight, you're in the wrong place. I've got a lasso, and I don't mind using it."

With a quick flick of my wrist, I swung my lasso at the woman, but as it neared her, something strange happened —the lasso went right through her. I stumbled back, surprised, as she laughed—a low, wicked sound that echoed through the fog.

"Now, hold on a minute," *I said, stepping back.* "You're no ghost. You're some kind of trickster, aren't you?"

The Veiled Lady let out another laugh, this time more melodic, before she raised her hand, and the veil fell back. The face beneath wasn't the face of a ghost at all, but of a young man—a boy, really, no older than sixteen, dressed in the most ridiculous black cloak I'd ever seen.

"Well, I'll be..." *I muttered.* "So it was you, huh? All these folks running around scared, and it turns out it's just a couple of kids playing a prank."

The boy, no longer hiding behind his veil, smiled

sheepishly. "Well, I didn't think it would get this out of hand," he said, looking around nervously. "We just wanted to scare a few folks, you know? My buddy and I thought it'd be funny. But... I didn't mean to get everyone worked up."

"Worked up?" I said, grinning. "You've got people changing their meeting times and wandering around with clubs and flashlights! You've got the whole town spooked! I almost got my rope tangled up in your 'ghostly' hands!"

He looked at me and sighed. "I'm really sorry, sir. It was supposed to be a Halloween joke, but I didn't realize it would go this far."

"Well, partner," I said, crossing my arms, "it looks like you and your friends got carried away with your little joke. But I'll tell ya what. You don't have to go scaring folks anymore. You're the Veiled Lady, alright, but now it's time for you to face the music."

The boy nodded, looking relieved. "I promise I won't do it again. Thanks for not making a big fuss."

"Well," I said, "next time you try a prank like this, maybe try it on someone who's not known for rope skills. And for heaven's sake, no more 'clawed hands'—that's just creepy."

CHAPTER 10: THE PHANTOM TRAIN OF WESTERN MARYLAND

Now, I've been around trains long enough to know they can carry more than just passengers and freight—they can carry memories, secrets, and sometimes, even ghosts. And when I caught wind of the Phantom Train of Western Maryland, I knew it was time for Pecos Bill to step in.

They say the Phantom Train runs along the old tracks near Frostburg, a town in the western part of the state, and it's been spottin' people in the dead of night for years. The folks who've seen it say it's an old-fashioned locomotive, steam billowin' from its smokestack, the sound of its whistle echoing through the hills, but there's one catch—it never stops, and no one ever gets on.

Well, when I heard the stories, I figured I'd head up there and see for myself. The tracks were quiet when I arrived, but the air felt thick, like a storm was just waiting to break. The moon hung low in the sky, casting long shadows across the rusted rails. There was something about this place, something that made the hair on the back of your neck stand up like a cattle prod.

I walked along the old tracks, listening to the wind rustling through the trees and the faint sound of the train whistle in the distance. Now, I'm no stranger to ghostly encounters, but something about this train felt different. It wasn't just a haunting; it was as if the land itself had swallowed up the train and its passengers, leaving only the memories behind.

I kept walkin' until I reached a small platform, where a few weathered signs marked the old station. The place was long abandoned, but I could feel the weight of history in the air. The old train station used to bustle with activity back in the day, but now, all that remained were the echoes of a time long past.

That's when I heard it—the sound of a train's whistle, distant but clear, like it was just around the bend. My heart skipped a beat. I had to see this for myself.

I stood still, my eyes scanning the horizon, waiting for the train to come into view. The wind picked up, and then, as if summoned by the air itself, the Phantom Train appeared from the fog. It wasn't like any train I'd ever seen. It was an old steam locomotive, covered in rust and soot, its light dim but steady, casting a ghostly glow on the tracks.

The whistle sounded again, echoing through the night, but there was something eerie about it—like the sound wasn't just a train; it was a warning.

I stepped forward, intrigued but cautious. The train didn't slow as it neared me—it didn't stop at all. It just rushed past, its wheels screeching on the tracks, the steam hissing and swirling in the night air. But as it passed, I noticed something odd—there were figures in the windows, ghostly faces staring back at me, their eyes hollow and their mouths frozen in silent screams.

I reached out, but the train was already gone, vanishing into the fog like it had never been there at all. The silence that followed was deafening.

I stood there for a moment, trying to make sense of what I had just witnessed. Was it a ghost train? A time-warp? Or just some trick of the mind? I wasn't sure, but I knew one thing for certain—whatever that train was, it wasn't just a relic of the past. It was something else, something far older and more mysterious.

I decided to follow the tracks for a while, just to see if I could find anything else that might explain what I had seen. As I walked, the air grew colder, and the fog thickened around me. The sounds of the night grew louder, and then I heard it again—the whistle of the Phantom Train, this time closer than before.

I turned around, my heart pounding in my chest, but there was nothing. No train. No lights. Just the thick, suffocating fog.

It didn't take long before I realized the truth: The Phantom Train wasn't something you could chase down. It wasn't about solving a mystery or making sense of the impossible. It was something that was beyond human understanding, a piece of the past that refused to stay buried. It was a reminder that some things can't be explained—they can only be experienced.

As I made my way back to Frostburg, the sound of the Phantom Train's whistle faded into the distance, and I couldn't help but wonder if I would ever truly understand what I had seen. But I knew one thing for sure: The Maryland Panhandle has more secrets than it lets on, and this one would remain just out of reach.

CHAPTER 11: THE SOMETUB VOYAGE ON THE C&O CANAL

It was a fine, misty morning when I decided to take a little inspiration from the Sometub voyage—a trip made by John Pryor Cowan back in World War I, where he traveled the length of the C&O Canal in a makeshift motorboat. Now, you're probably wondering: Why Pecos Bill? A canal boat? Well, partner, the way I see it, if a fella can ride across the wild west on horseback, then cruising through some Maryland fog in a homemade motorboat should be a breeze.

I got my hands on a rickety ol' boat that looked a little like it came straight out of the junkyard, with an engine so old it probably saw the light of day during the Civil War. But who's to say that can't make for an adventure, eh? I named the thing Pecos Tub, and off I went, gliding down the canal, just like Cowan did in his Sometub.

At first, the ride was peaceful, calm even—just the sound of water slapping against the boat and the occasional whoosh of the wind through the trees. But that peace didn't last long. No sooner had I made it past Williamsport than my engine started sputtering like a cat with a hairball. Not again! The motor choked and coughed, and before I could do a thing, it died right there in the middle of the canal.

"Well, ain't this just perfect?" I muttered, eyeing the stubborn motor. I tried to give it a kick, but no amount of cowboy magic was going to fix this old thing. There I was—stuck in the middle of the canal, surrounded by fog thicker than a bowl of oatmeal, with no land in sight.

I wasn't about to let a little engine trouble ruin my day, though. I got out and started tinkering with the motor, giving it a few good whacks with my boot. But just when I thought I had it fixed, I felt something moving beneath me—some kind of thud—and the boat lurched sideways. I jumped up just in time to see a massive snapping turtle the size of a dinner plate come up out of the water, eyeing me with what I swear was a look of pure malice.

"Well, now, you're a big fella," I said, eyeing the turtle, who looked like it had just as much interest in the boat as in my lunch.

The thing gave a menacing hiss, and I realized—I wasn't just stranded. I had myself a territorial reptile to deal with.

I grabbed my lasso and, in one fluid motion, threw it toward the turtle's shell, hoping to get it to go away. But this turtle? It wasn't no ordinary critter. With one snap of its jaw, it cut through the lasso like it was nothing but string.

"Well, that's just rude," I muttered, but I wasn't about

to give up that easy. After a quick glance around, I spotted a nearby dock. It wasn't much, but it was something solid—and, better yet, it wasn't a turtle.

I swung the boat toward the dock, but I could feel the tension in my gut as the motor sputtered again. This was gonna be close.

As I got within a few yards of the dock, the fog seemed to part just enough to reveal an old man sitting on the pier. He raised an eyebrow at me as I pulled the boat in, struggling with the engine.

"You seem to be having some trouble there," the old man said, crossing his arms. "I saw you pass by earlier, and I thought you might need some help."

"Well, you reckon so?" I replied, glancing at the turtle that was now back under the water, probably plotting its revenge. "This old motor of mine's more trouble than it's worth."

He nodded and shuffled over with a small toolbox. After a couple of minutes of work and a lot of grumbling from the old man, the engine roared to life again.

"Guess I owe you one," I said, tipping my hat.

"Guess so," he said, looking at me with a twinkle in his eye. "But next time, leave the tub at home. This canal's got enough ghosts of its own without you adding to the noise."

I thanked him, fired up the motor again, and continued my trip. The fog cleared, the boat hummed along, and I *couldn't help but grin at the wildness of it all. Sometub might have been a joke, but the adventure? Well, that was anything but.*

CHAPTER 12: THE SAVAGE RIVER RESERVOIR MONSTER

It was a fine, cool autumn evening when I decided to make my way out to Savage River Reservoir. Now, this place had been whispered about for years—stories of strange sightings, mysterious sounds, and, of course, the elusive creature that folks around here liked to call the "Savage River Monster." They said it was a great beast that lurked in the depths of the reservoir, something between a serpent and a giant fish, with glowing eyes that shined through the water like fireflies in the night.

But, partner, I wasn't about to be swayed by no local legend. Oh no, I'd heard these stories plenty of times before—people saw things that weren't there, and animals got misidentified in the dark. Still, there was something about the Savage River that got under my skin. It wasn't just the fog that seemed to roll in thick and low or the eerie silence that hung around the water. It was something deeper, something the locals whispered about when they thought no one was listening.

As I pulled up to the reservoir, the fog was already setting in. The air was cool, but the water, still and dark, seemed to pulse with a life of its own. The trees around the reservoir creaked in the wind, and the world seemed to hold its breath.

I'd just finished the Sometub voyage on the C&O Canal, and the trip had been... well, let's call it interesting. Between the mechanical failures, the territorial turtles, and the ghostly "Sometub" legend, I'd learned that sometimes the journey didn't go as planned. The reservoir seemed like a place that could teach me a few more lessons.

I unloaded my gear, packed light, and took a small boat out onto the water, feeling the weight of the stories around me. As I rowed, the fog thickened, and the night crept in like an unwelcome guest. I wasn't expecting much—just a quiet evening on the water to clear my head—but the deeper I got into the reservoir, the stranger things started to feel.

It wasn't long before I heard it—the unmistakable sound of something splashing in the water, a low, rhythmic sound like the movement of something large. I stopped rowing, straining my ears, and looked into the mist, waiting.

Another splash, this one closer. And then, in the distance, I saw it—two glowing lights beneath the water's surface, moving like eyes tracking me through the fog.

"Well, now, that's a little more than I bargained for," I muttered to myself, eyes narrowing. "I'm not here to chase no monster, but I reckon you're not gonna scare me off that easily."

The lights disappeared for a moment, and I could feel

my pulse quicken. Whatever it was, it was watching me. I grabbed my oars, ready to row, but before I could take action, the creature rose from the water.

It wasn't anything like what I expected—a serpent, a fish, or even a giant turtle. No, this thing was something else entirely. Its head was shaped like a cross between a crocodile and a wolf, with glowing yellow eyes that bore into me. Its body was long and sinewy, the color of the dark water, and its scales shimmered faintly in the fog. It was monstrous—silent and still, floating just beneath the surface like it was sizing me up.

"Now, I don't know what kind of creature you are, but you don't scare me, partner," I said, trying to keep my voice steady. "I've faced down bigger things than you."

Without warning, the creature lunged at my boat, splashing water high into the air. I barely managed to dodge it, and the boat rocked dangerously, nearly capsizing. My heart was pounding in my chest, and the monster's eyes were still locked on mine.

"Alright, enough of this!" I shouted, swinging my lasso. "If you want a fight, you got one!"

I threw the rope, aiming for the creature's neck, but it was too quick. The beast slithered back beneath the water, vanishing in the blink of an eye, and before I knew it, I was alone again—at least, I thought I was. The water rippled, and I could feel something watching me from below.

That's when I heard it—a low, deep growl, coming from the water. The creature wasn't finished with me yet.

I grabbed my oars, ready to make a break for it, but the fog was closing in fast, and the water around me started to churn violently. The creature surfaced again, this time with its jaws wide, ready to strike. The boat was rocking dangerously, and I could see the strength of the beast's movements—its tail lashing out, sending waves of water crashing over the sides.

I had to think fast. I wasn't about to let some oversized reptile take me down. With all the strength I had, I swung the oars against the water, creating a forceful splash that sent the creature recoiling. For a moment, it hesitated, and that was my chance. I kicked the boat into motion, rowing with everything I had toward the shore.

The creature followed me for a while, but as I reached the shallows near the bank, it seemed to lose interest. With one last growl, it disappeared back into the depths, vanishing without a trace. The water settled, and the fog seemed to lift just enough to let me see clearly again.

I pulled the boat onto the shore, my heart still racing. I didn't know what I had just faced, but I knew one thing for sure—there was something living in those waters, something older and wilder than any of us could understand.

"Well, partner," I said, shaking my head, "I reckon that's one for the books. A creature in the Savage River? Seems like that's a story worth keeping."

As I made my way back to the safety of the land, I couldn't help but laugh. Whatever that beast was, it wasn't going to keep Pecos Bill from chasing a little adventure. But next time? I'd be a little more prepared.

CHAPTER 13: THE DOGMEN OF THE ALLEGANY MINE

In the hills of Allegany County, where the coal mines run deep beneath the earth, there's a tale that gets passed around the local taverns every now and then—a tale about dogmen, or what the miners called the "Coal Hounds". Now, you may think this is just some fancy folklore made up to scare the new kids, but let me tell you, there's more to it than that.

The story goes like this—back in the early days of the coal rush, when the mines in Cumberland and Frostburg were working overtime to supply the growing country, there was a crew of miners who worked the deepest shafts of the Allegany Mine. These were tough men, the kind who didn't scare easy. But even the toughest miners began to get nervous when strange things started happening down in the mines. Tools would disappear. Strange howls echoed through the tunnels at night. And every so often, a miner would go missing—vanishing without a trace.

The old-timers, of course, chalked it up to the rough conditions of the mines or some kind of tragic accident. But the newer, younger miners? They had their doubts.

One night, a young miner named Johnny McCabe, fresh off the boat from Ireland, was sent deep into the mine on a solo task to check a tunnel that hadn't been worked in years. The crew had heard some strange noises coming from that tunnel, and no one was brave enough to investigate. So, Johnny, being the daring type, volunteered.

As he walked down the old, abandoned tunnel, he noticed something odd. There were large paw prints in the dust—paw prints bigger than any dog he'd ever seen. They weren't like the tracks of a normal hound; these were massive, like something straight out of a nightmare.

Johnny, not one to scare easily, shrugged it off and kept going. But the deeper he went into the tunnel, the more he could feel something was off. The air grew colder, and the hair on the back of his neck stood up. That's when he heard it—a low, guttural growl that echoed through the walls. Johnny turned around fast, but there was nothing there.

Suddenly, the growl came again—closer this time, like it was right behind him. He spun around, and there, in the dim light of his lantern, stood the Coal Hound—a giant creature, part wolf, part man, with glowing eyes and massive claws. Its fur was matted and dirty from the mine, and its teeth were sharp as the edges of the coal itself.

Johnny's heart raced, but he wasn't about to go down without a fight. He reached for his pickaxe, swinging it wildly at the creature, but the dogman was faster than he could imagine. It lunged, and with a swipe of its claws, knocked Johnny to the ground, sending his lantern flying. The light went out in a puff of smoke, leaving them both in total darkness.

Johnny was nearly ready to give up, but that's when something strange happened. Out of the corner of his eye, he saw a flash—a dark figure moving swiftly through the tunnel. It was another dogman, and then another. They circled around him, growling, but they didn't strike.

Johnny's instincts kicked in. He realized these creatures weren't just out for blood. They were protecting something —a treasure deep in the mine. As the dogmen backed off, Johnny scrambled to his feet, now more curious than terrified. He'd heard whispers of the "coal vein of riches" that had been rumored to be buried deeper than anyone dared to dig. Was it possible the dogmen were guardians of that very treasure?

With the creatures watching him, Johnny knew he had only one chance. He picked up his lantern, reigniting it with trembling hands, and waved it in front of the dogmen. To his surprise, they didn't move. Instead, they stepped back, parting like a pack of wolves. They allowed Johnny to pass, but their glowing eyes followed his every move.

He made his way through the tunnel, finding a hidden cavern where the coal veins glimmered in the light of his lantern. But there was no treasure—just a deep, black hole in the center of the cavern, a hole that seemed to suck in all light and sound. Johnny had no intention of sticking around to find out what was down there, and he quickly made his way back to the surface, with the dogmen following him until the entrance.

Johnny survived, but he never spoke much about what he saw in that cavern. The older miners, however, said he'd been marked by the Coal Hounds—they say he could hear their howls every time he walked near the mines. And after that night, the dogmen were never seen again, but their presence lingered in the shadows, guarding their secret.

To this day, no one knows exactly what the Coal Hounds were guarding, or why they were so protective of the depths of the mine. But if you listen carefully on a foggy night near the Allegany Mine, you can hear the faint sound of growls carried on the wind, like the hounds are still watching, still guarding the dark secrets beneath the earth.

Some say if you wander too close to that mine, you might just get a visit from the Coal Hounds yourself. And let me tell you, partner, they don't like to share their turf.

CHAPTER 14: THE APPALACHIAN WENDIGO

Now, I've faced a lot of creatures in my time—some terrifying, some downright strange—but the legend of the Wendigo gave me pause. It's a creature of the night, and its tale stretches back to Native American folklore, but it's more than just a myth. The Wendigo is said to be a spirit of insatiable hunger, a creature that's driven by a need to consume flesh, and once it starts, it can't stop. It's said to be cursed, a human who was turned into a monstrous, emaciated beast after committing unspeakable acts, and now it wanders the woods, driven by its need for more.

The Wendigo is a common tale in northern forests, but there are those who believe it has found its way into the Appalachian Foothills, feeding on the isolation and fear of the people living there. The legends say it's not just a creature—it's a force of nature, tied to the land, and once it's set its sights on you, there's no escaping it. It is a predator, and its hunger is never satisfied.

When I first heard about it, I wasn't sure what to think. I've faced everything from vampires to river spirits, and I wasn't about to let some hungry ghost send me running.

But the stories kept coming—whispers from locals who had heard strange noises at night, people who had gone missing in the woods, never to return. It was time for Pecos Bill to find out if there was any truth to the tale.

I rode into the Appalachian Foothills one chilly evening, the fog rolling in heavy over the mountains. The trees stood like silent sentinels, their branches twisting into the dark sky. The air was thick with the scent of pine and damp earth, and I could hear nothing but the rustling of the leaves and the distant howl of a coyote.

I made my way deeper into the woods, my boots crunching softly on the underbrush, keeping my eyes peeled. The deeper I went, the quieter the forest became. The birds had stopped singing, and even the wind seemed to hold its breath. It was too quiet—unnervingly so.

I set up camp by a small stream, my fire crackling softly in the otherwise silent woods. But even as the warmth of the flames spread through me, I couldn't shake the feeling that I was being watched. The hairs on the back of my neck stood up, and I kept glancing around, expecting to see something moving in the shadows.

That's when I heard it—the unmistakable sound of footsteps, heavy and deliberate, coming from the edge of the camp. The wind had stopped, and the rustling of the leaves grew quiet as the sound grew louder.

I reached for my lasso, slowly standing up, but when I turned around, there was nothing there. Just the trees, swaying gently in the breeze, and the faint glow of my fire.

I wasn't about to let my guard down. "Alright, partner," I muttered, "I've faced down more than my share of spooks, but I reckon this one's gonna be a bit different."

And that's when I saw it—the outline of something moving between the trees, too large to be any ordinary animal. It was hunched over, its body long and twisted, and as it stepped into the light, I could see its glowing eyes—a deep, sickly yellow that seemed to pierce through the fog.

It was the Wendigo.

Its body was skeletal, covered in thin, matted fur, and its teeth—sharp, jagged, and covered in the remnants of some past meal—glinted in the firelight. It was the embodiment of hunger, its breath ragged and heavy, its eyes locked onto me with a kind of feral intensity.

"Is that what you want?" I asked, taking a step back. "You want me for dinner, don't you?"

The Wendigo let out a low growl, its claws scraping against the ground as it stalked forward, its gaze fixed on me. I wasn't about to let it get the best of me. I knew how to handle beasts of this nature.

With a swift motion, I threw my lasso, aiming for the creature's neck. It let out a hiss, swiping at the rope with its claws, but I was faster. I yanked hard, pulling it off balance, but the Wendigo wasn't going down easily. It fought against the rope, snarling and thrashing, trying to break free.

"You've got the wrong idea, partner," I said, my boots sliding in the mud as I pulled harder. "I'm not your next meal."

The Wendigo's growls grew louder, more desperate, but I wasn't about to let it take me down. With one final pull, I managed to slam it into the ground, its body twitching as it tried to rise again. But I wasn't done yet. I tightened the rope, securing it, and slowly stood up, watching as the creature's movements slowed.

For a moment, I thought I saw something different in its eyes—regret, maybe, or just exhaustion. But before I could think more on it, the creature let out one last, bloodcurdling scream and vanished into the fog, leaving nothing behind but the rustle of leaves and the echo of its growls.

I stood there for a long time, catching my breath. The Wendigo was gone, but the woods still felt heavy, like the land was holding onto the memory of the creature.

"Well, that was a bit more excitement than I was looking for," I muttered to myself, tipping my hat. "But I reckon I'll sleep just fine tonight, knowing that I'm not the one on the menu."

CHAPTER 15: THE DISAPPEARING GANDY DANCER

Now, I've met a fair share of folks who work with railroads. Hard-nosed, no-nonsense types who know every inch of track like the back of their hand. But the tale I'm about to share isn't about the folks who work the tracks. No, it's about a man who vanished without a trace—someone who wasn't just a worker, but someone who seemed to know the railroads better than anyone else, and in the end, it got him into a mess he couldn't get out of.

It all starts with a man they called Gandy Dancer, and let me tell you, it's not a name you just pick out of thin air. Back in the late 1800s, Gandy Dancers were the nickname given to railroad workers who set the rails, lined them up, and kept everything running smooth. They had to be quick on their feet, able to dance around the tracks like they were waltzing with danger. But there was one particular Gandy Dancer who became a legend, and not for his work ethic.

His name was Jacob "Jake" McAllister, and he was said to be the best Gandy Dancer the Great Allegheny Passage had ever seen. He could lay track faster than a steam engine could run, and he always worked alone. He didn't talk much, but when he did, it was about the land, the tracks, and something else. Some say he claimed to hear the railroads calling to him, telling him secrets only he could hear. Others said he had a strange connection to the tracks, that he could predict where the train would go next, like some kind of supernatural power.

Now, I don't normally put stock in rumors, but when I heard about Jake's disappearance, I knew I had to investigate. The story goes that one night, Jake was working late, long after the last train had passed through. He was out near an old stretch of the railroad track, one of the most remote areas in the Allegheny Mountains. The crew went to look for him the next morning, but when they arrived, all they found were his tools scattered on the ground, his lantern still burning, and the sound of the wind howling through the trees. But Jake? Gone, like he'd never been there.

Some say the Gandy Dancer was taken by the land itself, that he was swallowed up by the very tracks he worked on. Others say he met some kind of mysterious fate, something no one understood. But one thing was clear—Jake McAllister vanished without a trace, and to this day, no one's been able to explain what happened to him.

I decided to find out for myself.

I rode up to the stretch of track where Jake had disappeared, the evening fog thick in the air, wrapping the trees and the earth in a ghostly blanket. The silence was deafening, broken only by the occasional creak of the tracks as they settled in the cool night air. The ground beneath me felt strange, as if the very earth was watching, waiting.

I walked along the tracks, my boots crunching against the gravel. There was no sound, no movement, but I couldn't shake the feeling that I wasn't alone. The fog seemed to cling to the tracks, and in the distance, I could hear the faint sound of something—the rattle of chains, the creak of wood, like an old train passing through.

I turned, my eyes scanning the darkness, but there was nothing there. Still, the sound lingered, echoing through the woods like a distant memory. Then, just as I thought it was my imagination, I saw it—Jake's lantern, flickering in the distance, swinging back and forth as though someone was carrying it.

I moved closer, my heart racing, and that's when I heard it again—the sound of footsteps, soft but steady, like someone walking the tracks in time with my own. I spun around, hand on my lasso, but there was no one there. The fog thickened, and the lantern continued to swing ahead of me, taunting me with its dim glow.

"Alright, partner," I muttered to myself. "I know you're out there. Let's see if you've got any tricks up your sleeve."

I moved closer, my steps cautious, but the closer I got to the lantern, the further it seemed to drift away. It wasn't running from me, but it was leading me somewhere, drawing me deeper into the fog. I followed, determined to uncover the mystery of Jake's disappearance.

The fog grew thicker, and the tracks twisted in ways that didn't seem right. It felt like I was being pulled into another world, one where the rules of the living didn't apply. The air was thick with the scent of damp earth and iron, and I could almost hear the faint sound of a train whistle, distant but clear, calling to me.

And then, just as I reached the lantern, it went out. The fog swallowed the light, and the world around me went completely dark. I spun around, lasso in hand, but there was nothing. No sound, no movement. Just the heavy silence of the woods.

I wasn't about to let that stop me. I pulled out my knife and cut through the fog with my senses sharp as ever. I'd been in situations like this before—staring into the unknown, but I wasn't about to back down. The train was coming, and I could hear it. I could feel the vibration of the rails beneath my feet, growing louder.

Suddenly, the ground shook beneath me, and I saw it—a shadow on the tracks. The Phantom Train of the Great Allegheny Passage, its ghostly form emerging from the mist, barreling down the tracks. And right next to it, I saw Jake, his ghostly form walking alongside the train, his face twisted in a grim expression.

"I reckon I've seen my share of ghosts," I said with a grin, "but a Gandy Dancer's ghost? That's a new one."

Jake's spirit turned to me, his face a reflection of his troubled past. But he wasn't angry. No, he was just lost, trapped between the world of the living and the dead. I didn't know how to help him, but I wasn't about to leave him to walk these tracks forever.

"Alright, Jake," I said, stepping forward. "Let's get you

off these tracks. You don't belong here anymore."

The fog cleared for a moment, and in the distance, I saw the full moon rising, its light illuminating the tracks. With one final nod, Jake's spirit faded into the mist, his presence gone as if it had never been there at all.

The Phantom Train passed by one last time, and the eerie whistle echoed in the distance. I stood there, breathless, but knowing I'd just helped another lost soul find its peace.

CHAPTER 16: THE MARYLAND HEIGHTS GHOST

Now, I've been through a lot of strange places, faced down more ghosts and monsters than I care to count, but when I heard the story about the Maryland Heights and the ghost of Private James Lancaster, I couldn't help but be intrigued. Folks say this place is haunted, but not by just any old ghost. No, this one's a soldier—a ghost who's been wandering the heights for over a century, still looking for the comrades he lost during the Battle of Harpers Ferry.

As the story goes, Private Lancaster was a young man, full of fire, stationed on the Maryland Heights to guard the river during the Civil War. But when the battle raged, he was caught between enemy lines and wounded badly. Some say he was left to die, others say he was just too stubborn to know when to quit, and when he died, they say the land kept him there, caught between the living and the dead.

Well, when Pecos Bill hears about a ghost soldier still wandering around, it doesn't take much to get me to saddle up and investigate. Besides, I wasn't about to let some restless spirit get the best of me.

So there I was, walking up the trail to the Heights, the sun starting to set behind me. The air was cool, the fog rolling in thick, like the land was holding its breath. The kind of night where things don't seem quite right. The kind of night you know something's out there, watching.

I made my way up, my boots crunching through the leaves, and I could feel it—the tension in the air. The fog closed in around me, and the trees looked like they were whispering in the wind. Something about this place felt wrong. This wasn't just a battlefield—it was a place where old ghosts never quite got the message to move on.

Just as I reached the top, I heard it. The sound of footsteps—soft but steady, like someone walking in my tracks. I stopped, hand on my lasso, and waited. The fog thickened, and the shadows around me seemed to move.

"Well, I reckon you're Private Lancaster," I said, my voice cutting through the stillness. "Or one of your pals. You'll have to forgive me, I don't usually make a habit of speaking to the dead."

A shadow moved out of the mist, and I saw him—the ghost of Private Lancaster, his uniform torn and tattered, his face pale and gaunt, eyes wide open but seeing nothing. He didn't speak, just stood there, staring at me like he was waiting for something.

I wasn't about to let a ghost stand there without getting some answers. "I reckon you're lost, partner. But I'm not one to stand around in fog with a stranger, so let's get this over with."

The ghost raised a hand, his fingers trembling, pointing toward the trees below the Heights. I followed his gaze, but there was nothing there—just the dark woods and the faint rustling of leaves.

"You're searching for something, aren't you?" I asked, narrowing my eyes. "Something you never found, something you never got the chance to do?"

The ghost nodded slowly, his gaze never leaving mine.

"Well, I reckon you've been wandering these woods long enough," I said, shifting my weight and preparing for whatever came next. "But you don't need to keep wandering. I'm not one to let a ghost take a long walk for nothing."

Suddenly, the ground beneath my feet shifted. A loud rumble echoed in the distance. The fog grew heavier, the temperature dropping fast. The air felt thick, like the land itself was trying to hold me in place.

"Alright, I see how it is," I muttered, tightening my grip on my lasso. "If you're gonna be stubborn about it, I guess we'll just have to do this the hard way."

The ghost's figure flickered in and out of existence, like he couldn't decide whether to materialize or vanish. With a deep breath, I swung my lasso through the fog, catching the ghost's outstretched hand.

The struggle was on. The lasso tightened around his form, and I could feel the coldness of his spirit fighting against me. The fog swirled violently, and the trees groaned like they were coming to life. For a moment, I thought the whole mountain might collapse under the weight of the past.

But Pecos Bill don't back down. With a sharp pull, I yanked the ghost closer, his body flickering like a dying flame, and I whispered, "It's time to move on, partner. Time to stop searching."

The ground trembled one last time, and with a flash of light, the ghost of Private Lancaster vanished, his form dissipating into the fog like a bad memory.

The silence returned. The fog began to lift, and the air grew still again. I stood there, catching my breath, knowing I'd just helped another lost soul find peace.

"Well, that wasn't so bad," I said with a grin, tipping my hat to the now-empty woods. "A little more fight than I expected, but I'm used to that."

As I made my way back down the trail, the fog parted, and the evening sun broke through the trees, casting a golden light over the land. The Maryland Heights, once haunted by the ghost of a lost soldier, were silent once again.

I reckon some ghosts are a little harder to deal with than others, but at least they don't keep me waiting too long.

CHAPTER 17: THE CACAPON RIVER SERPENT

The Cacapon River is like a dark, twisting ribbon running through the hills of the Maryland Panhandle. The locals know it well, and they know that it's home to a legend —one that's been passed down for generations. They speak of a great serpent that dwells in the depths of the river, a creature as old as the land itself. Some say it's a guardian, others say it's a curse. No one's ever quite sure, but the stories are enough to make any sensible person think twice before stepping too close to its waters.

Now, I've heard more than my share of tall tales, but when the legend of the Cacapon River Serpent reached my ears, I figured it was time to see for myself. I'd ridden through the area plenty of times, but I'd never stopped long enough to get a real feel for the place. That day, the air was heavy, the sky a thick blanket of clouds, and the river ran dark and quiet, like it was hiding something.

I made my way to the riverbank, the thick woods surrounding the water like a dark curtain. The trees seemed to close in around me as I approached, their branches twisting in ways that made it feel like something was watching. I didn't believe in superstitions, but I couldn't shake the feeling that something was different today. The river didn't just flow—it seemed to pulse, like the land itself was holding its breath.

I sat down by the bank and took a long, hard look at the water. It was still, too still, and I couldn't help but feel the weight of the stories—the ones about the serpent who could control the river, the one who dragged people under and never let them resurface. I had to see it with my own eyes.

Then, just as I was starting to think it was all nonsense, I heard it—a low rumble beneath the surface, like the river itself was alive. The air grew colder, the wind picking up, and the water began to ripple. I jumped to my feet, my hand instinctively going to my lasso.

I wasn't sure what I was expecting, but I wasn't ready for what happened next. The water broke with a violent splash as a massive head emerged from the river. Its eyes were glowing, yellow and eerie, and its scales shimmered in the dim light like oil on water. The serpent was enormous—bigger than any snake I'd ever seen, and it wasn't just a snake. This thing had the body of a serpent, but it moved with a speed that defied logic, its long tail thrashing through the water with the force of a mighty river.

I wasn't about to let it get the best of me. I had faced demons, outlaws, and monsters before, but this was different. The creature didn't just look dangerous—it looked hungry.

I reached for my lasso and threw it with all my might, aiming to catch the serpent's head. The rope landed around its thick neck, but the creature jerked its head violently, almost pulling me into the water. The river surged beneath me as the serpent fought against the rope, twisting and thrashing.

The tension in the air was thick, the sound of the serpent's growl mixing with the rush of the river. I pulled with all my strength, but the creature was too powerful. It wasn't just trying to escape—it was trying to drown me, to drag me into the depths of the river with it. My boots slid in the mud, and for a moment, I thought I might lose my footing.

But Pecos Bill doesn't give up that easily.

With one last heave, I yanked the rope tight, pulling the serpent's head toward me. It let out a hiss, but it was too late. The serpent, exhausted from the struggle, finally relented and slipped back into the river, its massive body disappearing beneath the surface with a final splash. The water settled again, but the eerie glow in its depths remained, like the creature was still watching.

I stood there for a long moment, catching my breath and watching the water. The Cacapon River Serpent had shown itself to me, and for a brief moment, I thought I might have been swallowed whole. But it was gone now, back in the depths where it belonged.

But as I turned to leave, I couldn't shake the feeling that it wasn't over. The serpent wasn't just a legend—it was something that had lived for centuries, something that knew the land and the water like no one else could. It might have retreated for now, but I knew it wouldn't be long before it surfaced again.

As I walked away from the riverbank, the feeling of being watched never quite left me. The Cacapon River Serpent was still out there, lurking in the shadows, waiting for the next fool to test its power.

CHAPTER 18: THE BANSHEE OF WASHINGTON COUNTY

Now, I've heard my share of eerie howls in the night, but nothing quite like the stories I heard about the Banshee of Washington County. Folks who've spent their lives here swear that on certain nights, when the wind is right and the air is thick with fog, you can hear her—a woman's wail that sends chills down your spine and makes your blood run cold. They say she's been haunting these hills for over a century, and that her cry is a warning of death, a harbinger of doom.

The tale goes like this: Back in the 1800s, there was a young woman named Ellen O'Reilly, who had moved to the area with her family from Ireland. Her father had been a proud man, strong and hardworking, but he was also a man with a temper. They say he had a falling out with the town over land, and it wasn't long before things escalated to violence.

One night, during a heated argument, Ellen's father was struck down by a mysterious figure in the shadows.

He was found the next morning, lying in the woods near the family home, and Ellen, distraught and lost in grief, couldn't accept his death. They say she blamed herself for not stopping the fight, and in her madness, she wandered the hills at night, wailing for her father, begging for his forgiveness.

But as the years passed, Ellen's grief turned into something else. It was said that she was taken by the spirits of the hills, and her cries became something more than sorrow—they became a curse. A wail that could be heard echoing through the mountains and fields of Washington County, warning the living of impending death.

I'd heard the story many times before, but I wasn't one to back down from a good challenge. So, when I found myself near Antietam Battlefield one misty evening, I decided to see if the stories were true.

As I walked through the fields, the wind picking up, I could feel the air change, like the land itself was holding its breath. The fog rolled in, thick and heavy, obscuring everything in sight. It was the kind of night that made you feel like you were walking in a dream—or a nightmare. I had a sense that something was watching me, following me, but there was no sound, no movement—just the wind and the creeping fog.

That's when I heard it—a faint wail in the distance, barely audible at first, like the cry of someone in pain. But the longer I stood there, the louder it became. It wasn't just a cry of sorrow—it was a wail of despair, sharp and mournful, cutting through the silence like a blade.

I spun around, hand on my lasso, and saw her—a figure

moving through the fog, her form almost indistinct, like a shadow caught in the mist. She was tall, dressed in a long, flowing gown, her hair wild and tangled, and her face was hidden by the mist, but I could feel her eyes on me. The wail grew louder, closer, until it seemed like it was coming from all directions at once.

I wasn't sure if it was the spirit of Ellen O'Reilly or something else entirely, but I knew one thing—this was no ordinary ghost. This was a force of nature, a wail that came from the very earth itself, warning of death and destruction.

"Enough!" I shouted, my voice carrying through the fog. "I don't know what kind of grief you're carrying, but I'm not afraid of you."

The wail stopped, and for a moment, everything was still. I could feel the presence of the banshee, like she was standing right in front of me, but I couldn't see her. The air was thick with energy, the fog swirling around my feet.

"Who are you?" I asked, stepping forward. "What do you want from me?"

There was no answer, only the sound of the wind. But then, slowly, the figure began to fade, disappearing into the fog as quickly as she had appeared. The wail, once so loud and sorrowful, faded with her, until there was nothing left but the silence of the battlefield.

I stood there for a long time, my heart still racing. The banshee's cry had been real, and though I couldn't explain it, I knew I had heard the warning of death. The land *of Washington County wasn't done with its haunted past, and neither was I.*

I walked back through the fog, the land feeling different now, as if it held more secrets than I could ever uncover. The Banshee of Washington County had delivered her warning, but whether or not I had listened was another matter entirely.

CHAPTER 19: THE LEGEND OF THE DEWAYO

Now, when I heard about the Dewayo, I didn't know whether to laugh or load up on extra gear. A wolf-like creature that walks on two legs and leaves cryptic footprints in the mud? Sounded like the sort of thing you'd expect to find in a ghost story, not in the deep woods of the Maryland Panhandle.

The Dewayo is a creature from the folklore of the region, and it's said to be a wolf-like being with a bushy tail, sharp claws, and a hunched back. It's reported to walk upright like a man, its eyes glowing in the dark, making it one of the more unsettling cryptids in the area. The stories say it's been spotted in the woods surrounding Frederick County, which is right on the edge of the Maryland Panhandle, but no one really knows what it is. Some think it's just a misidentified wolf or bear, while others claim it's something much more supernatural.

I wasn't about to let some wild animal spook me. So, one evening, I saddled up Widowmaker and made my way to the woods, determined to see what this creature was all about. The moon was high, casting pale light over the trees as I trekked deeper into the forest, my boots crunching on the leaves and the air thick with the scent of damp earth. The Appalachian foothills rose up around me like silent sentinels, and the further I went, the thicker the fog seemed to get.

That's when I heard it—the sound of twigs snapping in the distance, like something large was moving through the woods. It wasn't an animal, though. No, this sound was deliberate, like it was trying to keep its movements quiet. And then, the unmistakable sound of something walking on two legs—a slow, deliberate gait that was far too heavy to be a deer, yet far too quiet to be a man.

I stopped, my hand instinctively going to my lasso. I wasn't sure what I was dealing with, but I wasn't about to face it unprepared.

The rustling grew louder, closer, and then, from the fog, I saw it—a creature moving between the trees, its silhouette massive and hunched. Its eyes glowed faintly in the moonlight, two amber orbs piercing through the darkness. Its fur was thick and matted, its shoulders broad, and its body moved with a terrifying grace for something so large. But the most disturbing thing of all was the way it walked—upright, like a man, but with the savage strength of a wolf.

I froze, watching as it moved closer, its head turning slightly, sniffing the air. I could see the outlines of its claws as it reached out to swipe at a nearby tree, its nails scraping against the bark.

"Well, ain't you a sight for sore eyes," I muttered, my hand tightening on the rope of my lasso. "But I don't reckon *you're here to share a drink, are you?"*

The creature's eyes locked onto mine, and for a moment, I thought I saw a flicker of intelligence in its gaze. It wasn't just an animal—it was aware, calculating, and it didn't seem afraid of me.

The creature let out a low growl, its chest rising and falling as it sized me up. I could see its sharp teeth glistening in the moonlight, but I wasn't about to back down. If it wanted a fight, it was going to get one.

I took a step forward, my lasso ready, and I could feel the tension in the air. The creature's growl grew louder, more guttural, and before I could react, it lunged at me, its claws swiping through the air. I ducked just in time, the creature's claws grazing the top of my hat.

"Not bad," I said, grinning. "But I'm faster than you think."

I swung my lasso high and threw it with all my might, the rope landing around the creature's neck. With a sharp tug, I pulled it toward me, but it wasn't easy. The creature fought back with the strength of a wild animal, its claws scraping against the rope as it tried to break free.

"Well, you're a stubborn one, I'll give you that," I muttered, pulling harder. "But I've handled worse."

The creature let out a howl, its body thrashing violently, but I held on tight. It was like wrangling a wild bull, only this one had claws and teeth. I yanked the creature toward me one last time, using all my strength to pull it off balance.

With a final jerk, the creature fell to the ground, its claws scraping at the dirt. It let out a frustrated growl but didn't fight anymore. I stepped back, watching as it slowly retreated into the fog, disappearing into the night as quickly as it had appeared.

"Well, I'll be," I said, wiping the sweat from my brow. "That was a bit more exciting than I expected. I reckon you're not as hungry as you look."

With that, I turned and headed back toward my horse, the woods falling silent once again. The Dewayo may not have been a myth, but at least I knew it wasn't as fearsome as the legends made it out to be. Maybe it was just a creature caught between the human world and the wild, too stubborn to let go of the past.

CHAPTER 20: REFLECTIN' ON THE MARYLAND PANHANDLE

As I sit here, the moon hangin' low over the Maryland Panhandle, there's a peace that settles in me bones—like I've just come back from a long ride, but the ride's not quite over yet. I've faced some strange things in this land—creatures, ghosts, cryptids that lurk in the shadows, and even more peculiar tales that no one outside these hills would believe. But there's somethin' about this place, somethin' in the air, that calls to me. It's a land full of stories—stories that need tellin', and some that'll never quite be understood.

I reckon this land's been shaped by more than just time. It's been shaped by the people who've come and gone, and the things that lurk in the dark corners of the woods, down by the rivers, and deep in the forgotten places. From the eerie glow of the Hagerstown Ghost Light to the wails of the Banshee of Washington County, it's like the very ground here remembers every step, every footfall from the past. The Cacapon River Serpent and the Savage River Monster? They ain't just stories—they're reminders of a time when the world was wilder, and maybe that's why I'm so drawn to it.

I've met more than my share of creatures—some real, some real real in their own way. Like the Dewayo, that wolf-man who thought he could outwit ol' Pecos Bill with a little dance. He had rhythm, I'll give him that, but no amount of wiggling is gonna earn you the top prize when you're up against me. Then there was the Wendigo—talk about a challenge! I ain't one to back down from danger, but I gotta say, that creature's hunger was the kind that sticks with you. It was like the land itself had been twisted by greed, and I wasn't gonna let it take me down without a fight.

But even with all that, it's the Trickster of Wills Creek that sticks with me. That old spirit, with a laugh that could make the trees shake, challenged me in ways no cryptid or ghost ever did. He had the kind of tricks that make you stop and think: What's the real game here? Sometimes, I reckon we're all just a little too quick to look for the danger and not enough to look for the lessons.

And then, of course, there was the Veiled Lady of Williamsport—a prank played on a whole town, and I had to step in and fix it. Turns out the thing that's scariest in these hills isn't the ghosts or the monsters; it's a good ol' fashioned trickster spirit hiding behind a veil. A reminder that maybe, just maybe, we take ourselves too seriously sometimes.

But at the heart of it all, there's the C&O Canal, and the Sometub voyage. Now, that was a good, clean adventure—a little boat, a little mischief, and a lot of wonder. If you can't laugh at yourself while floating down a canal in a tub that barely holds together, well, partner, you're missin' out on some of the best parts of life. The folks who thought they were tellin' me about a "dangerous" boat ride didn't know that the real danger was in forgettin' to have fun.

Through it all, I've learned this: the Maryland Panhandle ain't just a land of monsters and ghosts, it's a land full of stories waiting to be told. It's a place where the past still lingers, where the fog hides more than just the land—it hides the memories of those who walked here before, the things they left behind, and the secrets they couldn't take with them. Some folks might say the dogmen of Allegany Mine or the Sideling Hill Phantom are just old tales, but I reckon they're more than that. They're the echoes of a world that's still shifting and changing, a world that's always got one more story to tell.

So, what's the takeaway, partner? What's the moral of the whole mess of adventures? Simple, really: Never stop exploring. Whether it's the depths of the Savage River Reservoir, the winding paths of the Catoctin Mountains, or the old forgotten places of the Maryland Heights, there's always something waiting. Maybe it's a monster. Maybe it's a ghost. Maybe it's just a good, old-fashioned trickster making fun of you. Whatever it is, you gotta face it. You gotta ride through it and laugh along the way.

And who knows—maybe in the end, it's not about finding all the answers. Maybe it's about the stories we gather, the friends we make, and the ghosts we put to rest. And don't forget, partner—there's always room for one more tall tale.

SNEAK PEAK

Pecos Bill Presents Peculiar Panhandles: Florida Tales

Well now, folks, settle in and grab yourself a lemonade because this tale is hotter than a skillet left out in the Florida sun. Let me tell you about the Legend of the Skunk Ape, a critter so ornery and elusive, it's said to be Florida's answer to Bigfoot. But where Bigfoot stomps through the forests of the Pacific Northwest with a gloomy sort of gravitas, the Skunk Ape is more of a tropical troublemaker. Some say he's a prankster, others a menace, but everyone agrees he smells worse than a wet dog rolled in swamp muck.

It was a humid summer evening deep in the Everglades, where the air is thick enough to chew and the mosquitoes are bigger than a Texas bullfrog. Old Widow Jenkins, the proprietor of the only bait shop for miles, swore on her mama's best cast-iron skillet that she saw the Skunk Ape clear as day. She was out back, tending to her moonshine still—purely for medicinal purposes, mind you—when she caught a whiff of something so foul it curled her hair tighter than a cowpoke's lasso.

"Bill," she said when she told me the story, "it was like

the worst outhouse you ever smelled, multiplied by three hurricanes and a dead fish."

According to her, the creature lumbered out of the mangroves, standing about seven feet tall and covered head to toe in matted fur. Widow Jenkins claims it paused for a moment, stared at her with eyes that glowed like swamp fireflies, and then tipped its hat—well, metaphorically speaking, since it wasn't actually wearing one.

I leaned in when she got to that part and asked, "Widow, are you saying the Skunk Ape has manners?"

She nodded solemnly. "Manners and a sense of humor. It swiped my best batch of moonshine and vanished into the swamp faster than a greased gator."

Well, now I couldn't let that slide. Not the moonshine theft and certainly not the insult to my legendary storytelling prowess. So I saddled up with a lantern, a net, and a bucket of fried catfish—because everyone knows the Skunk Ape has a taste for the finer things—and set out to find this elusive rascal.

What happened next? Well, you'll have to read the rest of the book to find out. Let's just say it involves a high-speed airboat chase, a misunderstanding with a couple of alligators, and a whole lot of swamp gas. But one thing's for sure, Florida may be flat, but its tales are anything but.

ABOUT THE PUBLISHER

Clover Fields Press

is an independent publisher based in Texas, dedicated to preserving folklore, history, and uniquely American voices. From tall tales and ghost stories to biographies and guides, we publish books that celebrate culture, spark imagination, and honor tradition. Learn more at CloverFieldsPress.com.

ABOUT THE AUTHOR

Clinton Lloyd Oberbeck

is an award-winning artist, multi-genre author, and US Navy Gulf War combat veteran. Visit the publisher's website to follow and read the author's complete biography.

Made in the USA
Coppell, TX
06 March 2026

73008685R00056